Open Wide

For Mandy and Ian, who have
the brightest smiles—N.K.

For Ben and Janet, who
keep us smiling!—J&W

GROSSET & DUNLAP
Published by the Penguin Group
Penguin Group (USA) Inc., 375 Hudson Street,
New York, New York 10014, U.S.A.
Penguin Group (Canada), 90 Eglinton Avenue East, Suite 700,
Toronto, Ontario, Canada M4P 2Y3
(a division of Pearson Penguin Canada Inc.)
Penguin Books Ltd, 80 Strand, London WC2R 0RL, England
Penguin Ireland, 25 St Stephen's Green, Dublin 2, Ireland
(a division of Penguin Books Ltd)
Penguin Group (Australia), 250 Camberwell Road,
Camberwell, Victoria 3124, Australia
(a division of Pearson Australia Group Pty Ltd)
Penguin Books India Pvt Ltd, 11 Community Centre,
Panchsheel Park, New Delhi - 110 017, India
Penguin Group (NZ), Cnr Airborne and Rosedale Roads,
Albany, Auckland 1310, New Zealand
(a division of Pearson New Zealand Ltd)
Penguin Books (South Africa) (Pty) Ltd, 24 Sturdee Avenue,
Rosebank, Johannesburg 2196, South Africa

Penguin Books Ltd, Registered Offices:
80 Strand, London WC2R 0RL, England

Text copyright © 2007 by Nancy Krulik. Illustrations copyright © 2007 by John
and Wendy. All rights reserved. Published by Grosset & Dunlap, a division of
Penguin Young Readers Group, 345 Hudson Street, New York, New York 10014.
GROSSET & DUNLAP is a trademark of Penguin Group (USA) Inc. Printed in
the U.S.A.

Library of Congress Cataloging-in-Publication Data is available.

ISBN 978-0-448-44439-0   10 9 8 7 6 5 4 3 2 1

Open Wide

by Nancy Krulik • illustrated by John & Wendy

Grosset & Dunlap

Chapter 1

"Emma, what are you doing?" Katie Carew asked her pal Emma Weber curiously. It was right after lunch on Monday, and Emma was by the sink in the girls' bathroom.

Emma opened her mouth to speak. White foam bubbled out around her lips. "'Rushing my 'eeth," she said.

"I know you're brushing your teeth," Katie told her. "But why here?" Katie had never seen anyone brush her teeth in school before.

"I had a cavity filled at Dr. Sang's on Saturday," Emma explained to Katie. "And I don't ever want to have another one. Dr. Sang told me to brush really well after every meal—

1

and that means lunch, too!"

Dr. Sang was also Katie's dentist. He was a nice enough guy. He was even kind of funny, the way he wore that weird smock with the pictures of teeth all over it. But Katie didn't like going to his office one bit.

First of all, there was the smell. The whole room stank of a mix of bleach and mint mouthwash.

The tube that sucked the water out of her mouth really grossed Katie out, too. Whenever it was in her mouth, she wound up drooling all over the paper bib Dr. Sang made her wear.

And then there were those black plastic glasses she had to wear when Dr. Sang took X-rays of her mouth. They always made her nose itch.

Basically, Katie hated going to the dentist.

"I never had a cavity," Katie told Emma. "Imagine—a hole in your tooth. Ugh!"

"Dr. Sang filled mine up with this silver-looking stuff," Emma told Katie.

She opened her mouth wide so Katie could see all the way in the back. Sure enough, there was a piece of silver inside one of Emma's lower back teeth.

"Wow! Is that real silver?" Katie asked.

Emma nodded.

"Did it hurt when Dr. Sang filled your tooth?" Katie asked her.

"Not after he gave me a shot to stop the pain," Emma replied.

Katie gasped. "A shot? *In your mouth?*"

"Yeah," Emma told her. "With a big, long needle. And then, when my mouth was all numb, he started drilling my tooth."

Katie gulped. She definitely didn't want to get a shot in her mouth. And as far as she knew, a drill was something construction workers used to put a hole in a wall, not something a dentist used in your mouth.

"It wasn't so bad," Emma told her. "And look what Dr. Sang gave me after it was all finished." Emma pointed at one of the belt loops on her jeans. She'd attached two key chains to one of the loops. Each key chain had a plastic tooth on it.

Katie agreed that the key chains were definitely cool. But they weren't cool enough to make it worth having a drill in her mouth.

"You know what? Starting tomorrow I'm bringing a toothbrush to school, too," she told Emma quickly.

"Cool," Emma replied. "We'll have a tooth-brushing party after lunch."

Katie giggled. "And tomorrow is the perfect day to start a tooth-brushing party."

"Why?" Emma asked her.

"Because today is Monday," Katie answered. "And that makes tomorrow Toothday!"

"From now on, *every* day is tooth day!" Emma exclaimed, placing her toothbrush back in its case.

Chapter 2

"Okay, watch me. This is my special runway walk," Suzanne Lock told the group of girls that were gathered around her on the playground after lunch. She lifted her head high, straightened her back, and took long strides across the yard.

Katie rolled her eyes. Her best friend was showing off . . . again.

"It's very important for a model to have her own special walk when she is modeling clothes," Suzanne explained. "A model has to stand out. At least a supermodel does. And that's what I'm going to be."

"More like a super*moron*," George Brennan

shouted as he and his best friend, Kevin Camilleri, tossed a football back and forth.

Kevin laughed. "And Suzanne won't have to practice for that," he said. "She's already an expert." He lifted his nose in the air, sucked in his cheeks, and imitated the way Suzanne was walking.

"Oh, that's beautiful," George told him, pretending to take Kevin's picture with an imaginary camera. "Smile for the camera!"

Suzanne stuck her tongue out at the boys. George and Kevin stuck their tongues out at Suzanne.

"Hey, you guys, throw the ball over here!" Jeremy Fox shouted to George and Kevin. He held out his arms and got ready to catch the football.

Kevin threw the ball, and in an instant the boys had switched their focus from Suzanne back to football.

Katie was glad. She hated it when kids fought or made fun of each other. If it were up to Katie, everyone would always get along.

"Can you show me how to walk like a model?" Zoe Canter asked Suzanne.

"Me too?" Emma Stavros asked. "That looks like fun."

Suzanne sighed heavily. "Modeling is not nearly as easy as it looks. It just looks that way when I do it because I'm so good."

"Please, Suzanne?" Zoe pleaded.

"Oh, all right," Suzanne agreed. "Now, just watch me and do exactly what I do." With each step, Suzanne stuck her right leg far out in front of her. Then she turned to face her friends. "Now you guys try it."

The girls did as they were told, Suzanne watching their every move.

"Emma S., stand up straight," Suzanne said. "Zoe and Katie, you're taking baby steps. Take giant steps . . . Emma S., a model can't look at her feet," she insisted. "She has to look at the . . . *oof*!"

Suzanne had taken a step backward and

smacked right into George, who was running
forward to catch the football. They crashed,
and George fell with Suzanne right on top of
him.

"Hey, Suzanne, watch where you're going!"
Kevin shouted.

"George should have been watching where

he was going," Suzanne insisted, getting up. "He crashed right into me."

"He was trying to catch a football," Jeremy told her. "You were the one walking backward."

Suzanne flipped her long brown curls behind her. "Come on, George, get up," she said. "Stop being so dramatic."

But George stayed there on the ground, holding his ankle. He gulped as if he was holding back tears.

"It hurts," he said through clenched teeth. "It really hurts."

"Oh, man!" Jeremy shouted. "I think you broke his ankle, Suzanne."

"I'll get the nurse!" Katie exclaimed. She zoomed into the school building as fast as she could.

A few moments later, Katie returned to the playground with Nurse Haynes. By now a whole circle of kids had gathered around George. The fourth-grade teachers, Mr.

Guthrie and Ms. Sweet, were making the kids give George some room.

Suzanne was standing off all by herself, watching. She looked upset.

"Let me through, guys," Nurse Haynes said as she pushed herself through the crowd of fourth-graders. "Okay, George, let's take a look." She bent down and gently examined his ankle.

"It's swelling up," Nurse Haynes noted. "I don't think it's broken, George, but you'll need an X-ray. Come on. We'll get you to my car."

Mr. Guthrie put his arms underneath George and scooped him up, taking care not to hurt his injured ankle.

"Don't worry. X-rays don't hurt a bit," Nurse Haynes assured George. "I'll call your parents and have them meet us at the hospital."

"Th-th-the hospital?" George looked really scared. "I've never been to a hospital," he said quietly. Then he glared angrily in Suzanne's direction. "All you do is cause trouble,

Suzanne!" he shouted. "I wish you didn't go to this school!"

Katie gasped. That was a terrible thing to wish. Katie knew better than anyone that wishes could be dangerous. Especially if they came true.

Chapter 3

Katie had learned *that* lesson the hard way.
It all started one horrible day back in third
grade. Katie had lost the football game for her
team. Then she'd splashed mud all over her
favorite jeans. But the worst part of the day
came when Katie let out a loud burp—right in
front of the whole class!

That night, Katie wished to be anyone but
herself. There must have been a shooting star
overhead when she made the wish, because
the very next day the magic wind came.

The magic wind was like a really powerful
tornado that blew only around Katie. It was so
strong, it could blow her right out of her body
. . . *and into someone else's!*

The first time the magic wind appeared, it turned Katie into Speedy, the hamster in her third-grade class. Katie spent the whole morning going round and round on a hamster wheel and chewing on Speedy's wooden chew sticks. *Bo-ring!*

She was sure glad she turned back into herself before anyone found out that it was really Katie, and not Speedy, who was in that cage with no clothes on!

The magic wind didn't just turn Katie into animals, though. One time it came and turned her into one of the Bayside Boys, her favorite musical group. She'd almost broken up the band!

One time the magic wind came to the Cherrydale Mall, and—one, two, switcheroo—it changed her into Louie, the owner of the pizza parlor. By mistake, she'd put cinnamon and sugar on the pizza instead of Louie's secret spice mixture! Actually, the cinnamon pizza tasted kind of yummy—like a big, doughy dessert. Louie thought so, too. He'd added it to his menu—although he wasn't exactly sure how he'd come up with the idea.

That was the weird thing about the magic wind. The people Katie turned into never really remembered much about what had happened to them.

But Katie never forgot. Which was why she hated wishes so much.

"Okay, everyone, let's line up and go inside," Ms. Sweet told the fourth-graders. "I think we've all had enough excitement for one recess."

The kids all did as they were told. As class 4A lined up beside 4B, Katie glanced at Suzanne. She looked kind of sick to her stomach—almost as if she were the one who had been hurt in the fall.

Chapter 4

"George, is this the bench where you want to sit?" Suzanne asked as she walked beside him the next morning in the school yard. She was carrying George's backpack for him. George couldn't carry his bag himself because he was using crutches to help him walk.

Katie stood nearby and watched with her mouth wide open. She couldn't believe it. Suzanne was actually being nice to George.

"No, I think I'd like to sit on that bench by the tree," George replied, pointing clear across the yard to a bench beneath a maple tree.

Suzanne grimaced slightly. "Okay," she

replied. "But remember, I'm carrying two backpacks—yours and mine."

"I can't carry my backpack," George reminded her. "I sprained my ankle when you walked into me yesterday . . . remember?"

Suzanne bit her lip. "I remember," she said as she headed over toward the maple tree.

"Do you believe that?" Katie asked Emma W., Becky Stern, and Mandy Banks as the girls watched George and Suzanne. "They're actually getting along."

"It won't last," Mandy predicted.

"What do you think is going on?" Emma W. asked.

"Maybe Suzanne feels guilty," Mandy said.

"Maybe. But you know what Jeremy always says?" Becky asked her. "He says that nobody ever knows why Suzanne does the things she does. I think he's absolutely right."

"You think *everything* Jeremy says is right," Mandy told her. "You have such a huge crush on him."

Becky's cheeks turned pink, but she didn't argue with Mandy. How could she? Everyone knew it was the truth. She reached into her pocket and pulled out a few squares of bubble gum. "You guys want some?"

"Oh yeah," Mandy said, grabbing one of the squares and peeling off the paper.

"Not for me, thanks," Emma said. "Chewing sugary gum can give you cavities. Besides, you'll just have to spit it out when we go inside."

"That's okay," Becky said, popping a square of pink gum into her mouth and chewing. "It loses its flavor in a few minutes anyhow." She blew a giant bubble.

"Good one," Mandy complimented her. She chewed for a minute and then blew a big bubble of her own.

That sure looked like a lot of fun to Katie. For a minute, she thought about taking a piece of gum, too. But then she looked over at Emma. And she thought about Dr. Sang and his dental drill.

No, Katie thought sternly to herself. She didn't want any holes in *her* teeth.

As Katie entered the cafeteria, Emma asked her, "Did you remember it's tooth day?"

"I sure did. I brought my travel toothbrush and toothpaste," Katie answered. Then she realized that Emma wasn't listening. She followed Emma's gaze and understood why.

George was seated at a lunch table, with his leg resting on a chair beside him. Suzanne was heading toward him with a tray of food.

"Okay, I got you the cheeseburger, the French fries, the ketchup, and the juice," Katie heard Suzanne say.

"Uh, Suzanne," George said, lifting off the top of the bun. "You forgot the little pickles on my cheeseburger. Could you go back for them, please?"

"But George," Suzanne said. "I'm really hungry."

"I'd get them myself, only . . ." George pointed to his bandaged ankle.

"Oh, okay," Suzanne said with a sigh. "I'll be right back with them."

Katie sat down in the seat across from George and pulled out her lunch. Her mother had packed her a really yummy Swiss cheese and tomato sandwich on a kaiser roll, and a fruit-juice box.

"Hi there, Katie Kazoo," George said, using the way-cool nickname he'd given her.

"Hi, George," Katie replied. "Is your ankle any better?"

"It still hurts," George told her. "I sprained it. The doctor said I have to stay off it for a few days."

"Suzanne's really being nice, huh?" Katie noted.

"She'd better," George replied. "She's the one who did this to me."

Just then Suzanne returned with the pickles. "Here you go, George," she said as she handed him a paper plate filled with thinly sliced pieces of pickle.

"What took you so long?" George asked her. "My burger is getting cold."

"Sorry, I bought my lunch while I was up there," Suzanne explained. She put her tray on the table and sat next to Katie.

"Hi, Suzanne," Katie greeted her.

"Hi," Suzanne answered. "Boy, am I hungry!" She picked up her cheeseburger and took a big bite.

No sooner did she begin to chew than George started to speak. "You know what this hamburger needs?" he said. "Mustard." He held his plate out toward Suzanne.

"I'll get it for you," Katie said, jumping up.

George shook his head. "Katie, you're a vegetarian. Looking at hamburgers probably makes you sick. Suzanne will do it."

"I don't mind," Katie assured him.

"I don't want to gross you out," George told her. "It would just make me feel bad."

Suzanne bit her lip and took the plate from his hand. "I'll do it, George, no problem."

Katie looked at her strangely. It didn't seem as though there was anything wrong with Suzanne. But maybe the fall yesterday did something to her head, because she sure was acting strangely!

Chapter 5

"I'll be a steady-ender!" Katie offered during recess as some of the fourth-grade girls gathered to play double-Dutch jump rope.

"Me too," Emma W. added, grabbing the other end of the two jump ropes.

Katie and Emma W. began twirling the two ropes one after the other. Katie smiled at Emma. Emma returned her grin, flashing her really white teeth right at Katie. Katie knew her teeth were just as white. After all, the girls had just brushed . . . and brushed . . . and brushed.

Katie looked down at the key chain with

the tooth attached to her belt loop. Emma had given her one of hers, because they were both members of the Pearly Whites Club. Emma had made that name up. Katie thought it was perfect!

"I'll go first!" Becky declared, leaping in between the two twirling ropes. "Teddy bear, teddy bear, turn around! Teddy bear, teddy bear, touch the ground . . ."

Katie stared at Becky with admiration. She couldn't believe how easily Becky was able to turn around and touch the ground without missing.

Katie always missed. She never seemed to be able to get the rhythm of the two double-Dutch ropes going round and round one after the other. That was why she always asked to be the steady-ender. Katie was really good at turning the ropes, even if she wasn't great at jumping.

"Suzanne, want to get in line?" Mandy called out across the yard.

At the moment, Suzanne was sitting on a bench next to George. He was reading a bunch of skateboarding magazines during recess.

"Sure!" Suzanne called out, jumping to her feet. "I just learned the greatest rhyme . . ."

"Oops, look what I just did!" George said as a whole bunch of plastic bugs fell from his jacket pocket. He looked down at the fake tarantulas, cockroaches, and worms that were scattered all over the blacktop. Then he glanced up at Suzanne and asked, "Could you pick them up for me?"

Suzanne made a face.

"They're fake, don't worry," he assured her.

"Okay." Suzanne bent down and began picking up the bugs.

"Be careful," George warned her. "Don't break off one of their legs or an antenna or something."

"Hurry up, Suzanne," Mandy called to her. "You can go after Jessica."

Suzanne looked longingly over at the jump-roping girls.

"You've got to get all the bugs," George insisted. "I don't want to lose any. I'd do it myself, but I'm not supposed to put any weight on my ankle, remember?"

"Can't Kevin or Jeremy pick them up for you?" Suzanne asked hopefully.

George shook his head. "They're playing football. They can still play football because no one knocked *them* over and sprained *their* ankles."

Suzanne sighed. "Forget it, you guys," she

shouted over to the girls.

As Katie watched her best friend picking up plastic bugs, she felt terrible. She knew how much Suzanne loved double-Dutch.

It didn't seem fair to Katie. She couldn't help thinking that George was really having fun making Suzanne feel so bad.

$$\times \quad \times \quad \times$$

When the bell rang at the end of the school day, Katie found Suzanne waiting outside the door of class 4A. That was weird, especially since Suzanne usually left school with the kids from her own class, class 4B.

"What are you doing here?" Katie asked.

"I got to leave early so I could help George carry his book bag home," Suzanne explained. She frowned and rubbed her shoulder. "I'm sore from carrying it to school this morning."

"I'll carry it for him," Katie told Suzanne. "I go right by his house on my way home."

"But I promised *I* would do it," Suzanne insisted.

"You've done enough for George today," Katie assured her. "It doesn't matter who brings his bag home."

"Katie, it's really heavy," Suzanne told her. "And besides, you're not the one who banged into him."

Katie smiled at Suzanne. "We don't have a lot of homework tonight, so there won't be a lot of books in his bag."

"Are you sure?" Suzanne asked her.

Katie nodded.

Suzanne smiled at her. "You're the best friend anyone could ever have!" she exclaimed. Then Suzanne ran off before George could stop her.

Chapter 6

"I don't know what happened to Suzanne," George told Katie as they left the school and headed for home. "She was supposed to carry my bag home."

"It doesn't matter," Katie replied. "I don't mind helping you."

"But that's not the point, Katie Kazoo," George said.

"How come your mom didn't pick you up in her car?" Emma W. asked. She and her little brother Matthew, who was in first grade, were walking part of the way with Katie and George. "That way you wouldn't have had to walk at all."

"I told her not to bother," George explained. "She's working today. She shouldn't have to leave work early just because Suzanne knocked me down yesterday."

"You know, George, it's not all Suzanne's fault," Katie told him.

"She wasn't watching where she was going," George reminded her.

"But you were running forward. That means you could see her coming. And you didn't get out of the way," Katie explained.

"Can I try your crutches, George?" Matthew asked.

George ignored Emma's little brother. "Katie, it all happened really fast," George insisted. "I didn't have time to move."

"You just didn't want to miss the ball," Katie guessed.

George frowned. "Whatever. I'm still the one who got hurt."

"Katie, does your mouth still feel fresh?" Emma asked, in an attempt to change the

31

subject. "Mine does."

Katie ran her tongue over her teeth. "Mmm. Minty."

"What are you guys talking about?" George asked.

"Katie and I are in the Pearly Whites Club. We brush our teeth after lunch," Emma explained.

"And we brushed them again right before we left school," Katie added, patting the tooth key ring Emma had given her.

"We're going to do it every day," Emma added. "No more cavities for me."

"Ooo, cavities," George said with a slight groan. "I've had two."

Katie didn't doubt it. Not with all the sweets George chowed down.

"Dr. *Fang* filled them both. It was horrible!" George continued.

"Dr. Fang," Katie giggled. "That's a good one."

"Man, I hate going there," George told her.

"The dentist is the worst."

"Uh, George," Emma said quickly, shaking her head. "Don't . . ."

"I know what you mean," Katie added, agreeing with George. "Don't you hate when he tells you to open wide, and then he sticks that metal pointy thing on each of your teeth?"

"Katie, could you not talk about . . ." Emma started.

"And how about that weird X-ray machine thing that goes all around your head?" George continued, ignoring Emma completely. "It makes the creepiest noise. And you're stuck in there. You're not even supposed to move!"

"Did Dr. Fang stick a giant needle in your gums when you had a cavity?" Katie asked him. "That's what he did to Emma."

"Uh—guys!" Emma said louder.

George nodded. "Uh-huh. And then he stuck this drill thing into my tooth. I could hear it digging. *Grrrrrr . . . grrr . . .*"

Suddenly, Matthew Weber's face turned bright red. Tears began streaming down his face. "I am not going to the dentist!" he declared angrily to Emma. Then he raced down the street ahead of them.

"What's with him?" George asked Emma.

"I was trying to tell you. He has to go to the dentist this afternoon," Emma told him. "He doesn't like going to any doctors. This is his first time at the dentist. And he was scared enough before you two started talking about it."

"Oh no! I'm so sorry, Emma," Katie apologized. "We didn't know."

"I tried to stop you from saying all that bad stuff," Emma explained. "But you guys just ignored me. Now it's going to be harder than ever to get him to go."

"Let me talk to him, Emma," Katie suggested. "I'll tell him we were just kidding."

"Forget it," Emma replied. "You and George said enough already."

Chapter 7

Later that afternoon, Katie sat in her room and tried really hard to do her homework. But she just couldn't stay focused on her two-digit multiplication problems. Her mind kept switching over to Matthew Weber.

Katie felt just awful about making Matthew cry. She hadn't meant to, of course.

Matthew was just a little kid. *A little kid who's afraid of the dentist.*

And Katie remembered exactly what that was like.

"Mom!" Katie called downstairs to her mom. "I have to go over to Emma W.'s house."

It was really important. When she got

there Katie would open her mouth really wide and show Matthew that she had no cavities. Then she would tell him that he would probably never have any, either—if he kept going to the dentist.

"You can go for a little while," Mrs. Carew replied, shouting up to Katie from the kitchen. "Be home by supper time. I'm making your favorite: vegetarian lasagna!"

Katie ran as quickly as she could toward the Weber family's house. She was hoping to catch Mrs. Weber before she drove Matthew to Dr. Sang's office. Katie rehearsed what to tell Matthew. "Going to Dr. Sang's office can be lots of fun," she said to herself. Okay, she didn't really believe that part. But she really wanted Matthew to believe it.

Katie rang the bell at Emma's front door. A moment later Emma's teenage sister, Lacey, answered it. Lacey was holding her one-year-old brother Tyler on her hip. Tyler's twin brother, Timmy, was standing next to them, sucking his thumb.

"Hi, Lacey," Katie said. "Are Emma and Matthew here?"

Lacey shook her head. "You just missed them. They left for the dentist's office."

"Emma went, too?" Katie asked her.

"Yep. Matthew insisted," Lacey explained. "He said she had to sit in the room with him and make sure Dr. Fang didn't stab him with a big needle." Lacey laughed. "Dr. *Fang*. I wonder where he got that from?"

Katie blushed and kicked at the ground. She knew exactly where he heard the name.

"I'll tell Emma you were here," Lacey told her.

"Yeah, thanks," Katie answered.

As Lacey shut the door, Katie sighed and started for home. Dr. Sang's office was too far away. Her mother wouldn't want her to go there all by herself.

The streets of Cherrydale were empty now.

No kids were playing ball or riding bikes.
They were all inside doing their homework.

Suddenly, Katie felt a cool breeze blowing
on the back of her neck. She used one hand to
lift up the collar of her jacket.

But the jacket didn't block out the breeze. It couldn't. After all, the wind that was blowing on Katie was no ordinary wind.

This was the magic wind!

Before long, the magic wind was blowing so hard, Katie thought she might be blown all the way across town. The magic wind picked up speed, blowing harder and harder until it was a wild tornado blowing only around Katie. She shut her eyes tight and tried not to cry.

And then it stopped. Just like that. The magic wind was gone.

And so was Katie Kazoo.

She had turned into someone else. Switcheroo!

The question was, who?

Chapter 8

Katie's eyes were still shut tight. Even though she had no idea who she was, she knew *where* she was.

It was because of the smell. Everywhere she sniffed, Katie could smell that bleach and mouthwash smell. There was only one place in the world that smelled like that.

She was in Dr. Sang's office!

Slowly, Katie opened her eyes and looked around. Sure enough, there were the big dentist chair, the bright lights, the toothpaste advertisements on the wall, and the collection of green and white plaster molds of kids' teeth.

What if the magic wind had turned her into Matthew Weber? Then she would have to go through his dentist appointment for him.

An extra dentist appointment! That would be the worst.

All of a sudden, Katie heard a boy crying out in the waiting room.

"I don't want to see the dentist!" he shouted. It was Matthew.

Okay, the magic wind hadn't turned her into Emma's brother. *So who was she?*

Katie looked down. She saw brown shoes and white pants. She was wearing a weird smock with teeth on it, too.

There was something a lot worse than being one of Dr. Sang's patients—

Being Dr. Sang!

And from the look of things, that was exactly who Katie had become.

Just then, the door to the office opened. Mrs. Shine, Dr. Sang's dental assistant, peeked into the room.

"Are you ready for your next patient?" she asked.

Katie gulped. She wasn't ready for the next patient. Or *any* patient! "Um . . . just a minute," she said. "I . . . um . . . I have to make a phone call."

"Okay," Mrs. Shine said, leaving the room. "Just buzz when you're ready."

As Mrs. Shine left the room, Katie sank back into her chair. Ready? How was she ever going to be ready to look into someone's mouth?

She glanced up at the clock on the wall. It was almost five o'clock. She was never going to get home in time for dinner. On top of everything else, her mother was going to be mad at her. She had to do something.

Quickly, Katie picked up the phone and dialed her own number.

"Hello," her mom answered the call.

"Hi, mom." Katie gulped. She'd forgotten

she was Dr. Sang now. "I, uh, I mean, hello, Mrs. Carew."

"Who is this?" Mrs. Carew asked.

"It's Dr. Sang," Katie told her. "I . . . um . . . I have Katie here in the office."

"What's she doing there?" Mrs. Carew wondered.

"She came with Emma and her brother," Katie answered. "And I was thinking, as long as I have her here, maybe she could have a checkup as well."

"Well, I suppose, if she wants one . . ." Mrs. Carew said. She sounded very confused.

Her mom knew how much she hated going to the dentist. This conversation probably sounded pretty weird to her.

But not nearly as weird as the truth would sound, Katie figured.

"Great," Katie said. "I'll call you when we're finished."

As she hung up the phone, Katie breathed a big sigh of relief. She'd bought herself some time, anyway. She leaned forward and rested her elbows on the desk. All of a sudden she heard a loud buzzing noise.

A moment later, Mrs. Shine entered the room with Emma at her side. Emma was dragging Matthew by the arm.

"You buzzed, and here we are," Mrs. Shine said.

Katie frowned. She hadn't meant to do that.

"Come on, Matthew," Emma urged her brother. "Going to the dentist is no big deal."

"George said Dr. Sang drilled in his mouth," Matthew reminded her. "Like the men do to make big holes in the street."

"It's not that kind of drill," Emma assured him. "It's tiny. And they only use it if you have a cavity. You probably won't have any."

"Hi, Dr. Sang," Emma greeted Katie.

"Hello, Emma. How's the tooth feeling?" Katie asked her. She was trying to sound like a real dentist.

"Great," Emma replied.

"And did you and Katie have fun at your Toothday party today?" Katie continued.

Emma stared at her in surprise. "How did you know about that?"

Oops. There was no way the *real* Dr. Sang could know about that. He hadn't been in the girls' bathroom when they were brushing their teeth.

"I . . . um . . . I'm a dentist. I get all the

tooth news," Katie replied quickly.

Emma looked at her strangely. But before she could say anything, Matthew tugged at Emma's arm.

"Can we go now?" he asked. "I wanna go home."

"Maybe we should do this another day," Katie suggested eagerly. If Matthew went home, Katie wouldn't have to stick her hands in Matthew's mouth and touch his tongue and his teeth. Touching someone else's teeth seemed really gross!

"Oh, no!" Emma exclaimed. "We can't do that. It was hard enough getting Matthew here this time."

"I don't know," Katie told her. "Maybe I should tell your mother to take him home. Where is she?"

"She's parking the car," Emma explained. "And I know she wants to get this appointment over with as quickly as possible. Matthew has been driving us all nuts!"

"I WANNA GO HOME!" Matthew shouted out, as if to prove it.

"Why don't you climb up into this chair first?" Mrs. Shine suggested gently. She lifted Matthew up and placed him in the dental chair. Then she used her foot to move a small lever at the bottom of the chair. "See how it moves up and down?"

Matthew nodded.

"Isn't that cool?" Emma asked him.

"Sorta," Matthew mumbled.

"I always like that part," Katie said. "Um. I mean, all my patients like to ride in the chair."

Mrs. Shine stared at her strangely. Then she turned her attention back to Matthew. "Now I'm just going to place this paper bib around your neck," she continued.

"No bib!" Matthew exclaimed, pushing her hands away. "Those are for Timmy and Tyler."

"Oh, this isn't a baby bib," Mrs. Shine assured him. "It's for big boys. We just want to keep your handsome shirt nice and dry."

Matthew frowned, but he let her put the paper bib on him.

"Okay now, open wide. Let Dr. Sang take a peek at your teeth," Mrs. Shine told Matthew.

Matthew clenched his teeth tight.

Katie knew just how he felt. She hated when Dr. Sang poked around in her mouth. And when she was little, she clenched her mouth shut the same way.

But she was the dentist now. And that meant she had to get Matthew to open his mouth.

Suddenly, Katie's eyes fell on a white sock puppet. It had big button eyes, an orange button nose, bright red lips made of felt, and big white cardboard teeth.

Quickly, Katie raced over and put the puppet on her hand. "Hi there, I'm Flossie," she made the puppet say. "What a nice smile you have, Matthew."

Matthew just sat there with his arms

crossed and his teeth clenched tight.

Katie frowned. This wasn't going very well.

"You want to hear a joke?" she made Flossie the sock puppet ask Matthew. "What did the tooth say when the dentist left the room?"

"What?" Matthew asked through his clenched teeth.

"Fill me in when you get back," Katie said. She laughed. Emma and Mrs. Shine laughed, too.

"I don't get it," Matthew insisted.

"You know, the tooth wants to be *filled* in. Like a cavity," Katie explained.

"A cavity!" Matthew exclaimed, leaping out of the chair. "The kind you use a drill for?" He burst into tears.

Katie frowned. This was *so* not good.

Chapter 9

"Dr. Sang, I don't think it's a good idea to joke with Matthew," Mrs. Shine whispered.

"I . . . um . . . I guess I wasn't thinking," Katie replied.

Mrs. Shine shook her head slightly. It was obvious that she noticed that Dr. Sang was acting kind of odd. She just didn't know why.

And Katie sure wasn't going to tell her!

Mrs. Shine turned her attention to Matthew. "You know," she told him, "I have some really great prizes in my desk. But they're only for brave children who let Dr. Sang look at their teeth."

"P-p-prizes?" Matthew asked, stopping

his crying and gasping for air. "What kind of prizes?"

"Things I think you'll like," Mrs. Shine told him. "But you only get to pick one if you hop back into that chair."

"Okay," Matthew agreed. He climbed back into the big dental chair and leaned his head back.

"Good boy," Mrs. Shine said. "Now, I'm just going to run out to the waiting room so when your mom gets here, I can tell her we've gotten started."

"But you're coming back, right?" Matthew asked nervously.

Katie frowned. Matthew liked Mrs. Shine better than he liked her. That kind of hurt her feelings.

"Of course," Mrs. Shine assured him with a smile as she left the office. "And your big sister is going to stay here with you, too."

"That's right," Emma told him. "I'm not going anywhere."

Katie bit her lip nervously. Now she was really going to have to look into Matthew's mouth and pick at his teeth. She was going to have to act like a real dentist.

How hard could it be? After all, Dr. Sang had examined Katie's mouth lots of times. She'd just do what he did.

That meant putting on those rubber gloves. Katie reached into the box and pulled out a pair. Then she took one of Dr. Sang's paper masks and put it over her mouth and nose.

"Okay, Matthew, open wide," she said.

Matthew opened his mouth. Katie looked down at the tray of dental tools Mrs. Shine had laid out for Dr. Sang. Now which one did Dr. Sang usually use first?

Oh, yeah. That round-mirror-on-a-stick thing.

Katie picked up the tool and stuck it in Matthew's mouth. But she still couldn't see his teeth really well.

"Wow, it sure is dark in there!" Katie

shouted into Matthew's mouth.

"You forgot to turn on the light," Emma
said, pointing to the big overhead lamp.

"Oh, yeah," Katie said, blushing. "Sorry."
She reached up and turned on the light. "Oh,
that's better!"

"Ach ite is koo grite," Matthew said.

"What?" Katie asked him.

"Ach ite is koo grite," he repeated.

"Sorry, I don't understand you," Katie said.

Matthew closed his mouth suddenly.

"Ow!" Katie shouted, yanking her hand out of Matthew's mouth. "You bit my finger!"

"The light is too bright," Matthew said. "I didn't mean to bite you. It's just that I had to close my mouth to talk."

Katie frowned. Dr. Sang always understood what she said when her mouth was wide open. Maybe it was something dentists learned in dental school.

"Well, close your eyes," Katie told Matthew as she shook her finger a little until the bite pain went away. "And open wide. Then afterward you'll get your prize."

Matthew did as he was told.

Once again, Katie stuck the mirror on a stick into Matthew's mouth and began to look around. She made a face as she examined his back teeth. There was a piece of corn stuck between two of the teeth, and a little bit of gummy candy on another tooth.

"Ick," Katie remarked. "How gross."

Emma stared at her in surprise. "Dr. Sang! That's not nice," she hissed.

Katie blushed again. Emma was right. That had been kind of mean. But it just popped out.

"I meant to say that I'm just going to clean out these back teeth," she said quickly. She took the mirror out of Matthew's mouth.

She thought for a moment. How could she get the food out of Matthew's teeth? At home, she used a water pick to clean out the food in her own mouth. Maybe Dr. Sang had one of those.

Katie looked around the chair for a moment. Sure enough, there was a water pick attached to the small sink on the side of the chair. "We'll just use this," she told Matthew, as she picked up the water pick and turned the knob to "on."

"AAAAHHHHH!" Matthew screamed as a blast of icy cold water hit him in the eye.

Matthew's scream shocked Katie. She jumped backward with surprise. When she did, she accidentally stepped on the lever that moved the dental chair up and down.

"WHOAAAA!" Matthew shouted as the chair shot up in the air.

Bam! He flew out of the chair and landed right on his rear end.

"I'm outta here!" Matthew screamed. He went for the door.

"Matthew, wait!" Emma cried out.

"Don't go!" Katie shouted. She leaped in front of the door to block his path.

Matthew tried ducking under her arm, but Katie stopped him.

Matthew turned and ran back to the dental chair. He grabbed the water pick. Then he shot a big stream of water across the room.

"Hey, stop that!" Katie shouted. She let go

of the doorknob to wipe her face.

Matthew zoomed across the room, opened the door, and darted into the waiting room.

"Matthew, come back!" Emma cried, running after him.

"I'm never coming back," Matthew insisted. "I don't care about the prize!"

Chapter 10

Katie stood there for a minute, alone in Dr. Sang's office. She couldn't believe what she had just done. Matthew had really freaked out.

He'd probably never go to the dentist again. And not just to Dr. Sang, either. Any dentist. His teeth would get all gross and full of cavities. Then they would all fall out. Not just his baby teeth, either. Even his grown-up teeth would rot out of his mouth. And when he grew up, he'd have to wear those fake teeth she saw on TV commercials.

And it was all her fault.

Katie felt terrible. She could hear Mrs.

Shine trying to comfort Matthew in the waiting room. But Matthew was still crying.

Katie shut the door and sat down on the big chair. Yuck! The seat was all wet. What a mess!

Just then, Katie felt a familiar breeze on the back of her neck. She didn't even bother to see if any windows were open or if the overhead fan was turning.

She knew it wasn't that kind of wind.

This was the magic wind.

The magic wind grew stronger, circling around Katie. The tornado whipped around wildly. It was so powerful that Katie was sure it was going to blow her away.

And then it stopped. Just like that.

The magic wind was gone. Katie was back.

So was Dr. Sang. He was standing right beside her. And boy, did he look confused!

"Katie," he murmured, rubbing his eyes and shaking his head. "What are you doing here?"

"I . . . um . . . I just blew by to see if Emma needed any help with Matthew," Katie explained. *There. That wasn't exactly a lie.*

"Matthew Weber?" Dr. Sang repeated. "Oh, yes. I think he . . ." Dr. Sang stopped for a moment and felt the seat of his pants. "Why am I wet?" he wondered out loud.

"You sat in the chair," Katie told him. "And there's water on it from when you sprayed that water-pick thingy in Matthew's mouth."

"I did?" Dr. Sang asked her. He blinked his eyes hard, trying to remember. "I guess I did. I kind of remember it. It's all sort of blurry."

Just then the door flew open. Emma's mother stormed into the office. "Dr. Sang!" she exclaimed. "What happened in here? Matthew says you blasted him with water and sent him flying out of the chair."

"Are you okay, Dr. Sang?" Mrs. Shine asked him as she followed Mrs. Weber into the room.

"Not really," Dr. Sang admitted.

"Well, I'm not okay, either," Mrs. Weber

told him angrily. "Matthew is refusing to go to the dentist ever again. What am I supposed to do about that?"

"I'm not exactly sure. This has never happened here before. I'm usually so great with kids." Dr. Sang looked very upset.

Now Katie felt even worse. She didn't love going to the dentist, but the funny thing was, once she got there, she always realized it wasn't all that bad.

If only there was a way Matthew could see that, too.

Suddenly a big wave of braveness washed over Katie. She knew exactly what to do.

"I can show Matthew it's not so scary," Katie assured Mrs. Weber.

"I don't think so, Katie," Mrs. Weber said. Then she paused. "Wait a minute. How did you get in here?"

"That's what I was wondering," Dr. Sang said. "She told me she just blew in to help with Matthew."

"You were so busy running after Matthew, you didn't see me come in," Katie told Mrs. Weber quickly. "Anyway, I really think I can help. All you have to do is get Matthew to stand in the doorway and watch. Dr. Sang and I will do the rest."

"We will?" Dr. Sang asked her.

"Uh-huh." Katie nodded. Then she took a

deep breath and jumped up into the big dental chair. "I'm going to have my teeth checked while Matthew watches. That way he'll see it's not so bad."

"Hmmm. You know, that just might work," Mrs. Weber said.

"I think so, too," Dr. Sang agreed. He smiled and picked up a clean mirror on a stick. "Okay, Katie, open wide."

Chapter 11

"Boy, Katie, that was great, what you did," Emma W. said as she and Katie walked through the mall on Saturday afternoon. "Matthew wasn't scared after he saw Dr. Sang give you your exam. He even asked my mom to get him a toy dentist kit for his birthday."

"Dr. Sang told me I might have to get braces in a year or so," Katie said.

"Oh, braces are cool," Emma assured her. "Lacey had them. She got to pick different colors for the wires. One month she had blue and pink. For Halloween she had orange. And then for Christmas she changed the colors to green and red."

"That does sort of seem like fun," Katie admitted. "If Suzanne ever needs braces, she'll probably try to get *glittery* wires."

Emma giggled. "Where is Suzanne, anyway?"

"She's around here somewhere," Katie said. "With George. He needed her to carry some packages."

"She's really been nice about helping George," Emma remarked. "She carried his books to school every day this week and got his lunch for him, too. I heard she even did his spelling homework on Thursday because his ankle hurt so much, he couldn't think."

Katie frowned. How could a pain in his ankle affect George's brain? And George was supposed to do his own homework.

"It's taking his ankle a long time to heal," Emma continued. "It's been almost a week now."

"I know," Katie agreed. "And it's weird because his mom told my mom that it really wasn't a bad sprain."

Just then, Katie spotted George standing outside of Hot Stuff, a store that sold really cool things like rubber bracelets, funky T-shirts, and rubber chickens. George was all by himself. And he was standing without his crutches.

"Oh look, George must be feeling better," Katie said happily. She waved in his direction.

As soon as George spotted Katie, he got a pained look on his face. Then he began limping over to a nearby bench.

Katie stared at George for a minute. Something wasn't right. "Hey, Emma, which ankle did George sprain?" she asked.

"His left one. Why?" Emma answered.

"Because he's limping like it's his right ankle that's hurting," Katie noted.

"Do you think he's faking it?" Emma said.

Before Katie could answer, Suzanne came stumbling out of Hot Stuff. She was carrying three heavy bags.

"Okay, George," Katie heard Suzanne say. "We've got everything you came to the mall for—even the big bottle of floor wax we bought before when we went to the cleaning-supply store."

"I told my mom I would pick that up for her as a favor," George explained. "She was nice to drive us here. I didn't think she should have to carry around that heavy bottle of floor wax, too."

"But *I* should?" Suzanne demanded.

George looked down at his ankle. "Well, I certainly can't carry it."

Katie frowned when she heard that. George was being really mean to Suzanne. She had a feeling Emma was right now. George was faking having a hurt ankle.

But how could she prove it?

"You know, I still want that hot dog and French fries," Katie overheard George say.

"Okay, so let's go over to the food court," Suzanne suggested.

George sighed. "The food court is so far away. Can't you go get my lunch for me?"

Food! That was it! Katie knew exactly how to prove George was faking his injury! Quickly, she hurried over to the bench where he was sitting.

"Hi, George. Hi, Suzanne," she said, plopping down on the bench next to George.

"Hi, you guys," Suzanne sadly greeted Katie and Emma.

"Suzanne, you look exhausted," Emma told her.

"Well, George has sort of had me running around and carrying a bunch of things," Suzanne explained.

"Wow. That's awful," Katie said sincerely.

"Hey, what about me?" George demanded. "I'm the one who was hurt."

Katie kept talking to Suzanne. "Did you see the black-and-white hair clips they have inside Hot Stuff?"

"No," Suzanne said. "But I didn't get a

chance to look at anything *I* wanted."

"Come on," Katie said. "I'm sure George won't mind."

"Yes, I would," George said. "Suzanne was going to get me lunch."

"This will just take a minute," Katie assured him.

As the three girls walked toward the store, Katie began to speak loudly. She wanted to make sure George heard every word.

"Guess what!" Katie said to Emma and Suzanne. "They're having a hot-dog-eating contest in the food court. The first ten people to show up get all the hot dogs they can eat for free!"

Katie made the girls turn around. George was already running off in the direction of the food court—without his crutches!

"His ankle's fine!" Suzanne exclaimed angrily. "He was just using me!"

"Don't worry," Katie told her. "He'll get his. There is no hot-dog-eating contest. I made

that up. Boy, is he going to be disappointed."

"That's not all he's going to be! Just wait until I get ahold of him." Suzanne ran off after George, waving her fists in the air.

Katie laughed. She sure wouldn't want to be George when Suzanne caught up to him.

Come to think of it, Katie didn't want to be anyone but Katie. Hopefully, the magic wind would stay away for a while. She wasn't in the mood for another switcheroo. She was having far too much fun just being Katie Kazoo!

Tell the Tooth

These are Dr. Sang's favorite tooth facts. And they're all the complete and total tooth!

1. Sharks lose teeth each week. They get new teeth when they lose the old ones. They may grow over twenty thousand teeth in a lifetime.

2. Your teeth start forming even before you are born.

3. The elephant's tusks are the longest teeth in the world.

4. George Washington's false teeth weren't made of wood. However, he did have sets of dentures made from hippopotamus teeth, cow teeth, and sheep teeth.

5. Dolphins have more teeth than any other animal. Some dolphins have over two hundred teeth.

6. The hardest thing in your whole body is the enamel on your teeth.